Powerslide

Jeff Ross

orca sports

ORCA BOOK PUBLISHERS

Library and Archives Canada Cataloguing in Publication

Ross, Jeff, 1973-
Powerslide/ Jeff Ross.
(Orca sports)

Issued also in electronic format.
ISBN 978-1-55469-914-8

I. Title. II. Series: Orca soundings
PS8613.R367B12 2011 JC813'.6 C2010-908062-9

I. Title. II. Series: Orca sports
PS8635.O6928P69 2011 JC813'.6 C2011-903343-7

First published in the United States, 2011
Library of Congress Control Number: 2011929397

Summary: Complications arise when Casey gets hired as a skateboarding double and a competitor challenges him to a series of dangerous tricks.

Orca Book Publishers is dedicated to preserving the environment and has printed this book on paper certified by the Forest Stewardship Council®.

Orca Book Publishers gratefully acknowledges the support for its publishing programs provided by the following agencies: the Government of Canada through the Canada Book Fund and the Canada Council for the Arts, and the Province of British Columbia through the BC Arts Council and the Book Publishing Tax Credit.

Cover photography by dreamstime.com
Author photo by Simon Bell

ORCA BOOK PUBLISHERS
PO Box 5626, Stn. B
Victoria, BC Canada
[illegible]

ORCA BOOK PUBLISHERS
PO Box 468
Custer, WA USA
[illegible]

[illegible]

Printed and bound in Canada.

14 13 12 11 • 4 3 2 1

For Megan and future skaters,
Luca and Alex.

chapter one

You need two things to be a good skateboarder: amazing balance and a complete lack of fear. Which was why I was surprised when Goat landed a 360° heel flip during our game of S.K.A.T.E. Goat had a lack of fear. He had proven that many times, but his balance was always slightly off. When it came to riding half-pipes, he usually landed badly. Yet he managed to land this particular 360° heel flip without a wobble.

I'll be the first to admit he nailed it. Not that I would tell him that. Goat and I had been competing against one another since we were ten years old and first started rolling around on skateboards. But this game of S.K.A.T.E. meant more than any of the others had. S.K.A.T.E. is a simple game. The first skater does a trick of their choice. The second skater then has to do the trick too. If the second skater lands the first skater's trick, the game moves forward and it becomes the second skater's turn to choose the next trick. If either of the contestants cannot land a trick, they get a letter. The first one to spell *skate* loses.

The question wasn't whether I could land the 360° heel, but whether I could pull off the 720° melon I planned to do on the other side. Goat was able to keep up with me on most tricks, but he had consistently been unable to land a 720° melon. Normally I wouldn't have cared, but today Jack Coagen was sitting beside me on the ramp. Jack is one of those big-name teen actors. If he stars in a movie, parents feel safe sending their rug rats off to the theater. He's at my neighborhood half-pipe because he landed the lead role in a feature film that happened to have some skateboarding in it. His agent wanted him to learn some basic skateboarding skills, so after he saw a video of me on YouTube, he contacted me to see if I could train Jack.

It's hard to teach someone to skateboard. Hard enough that, at first, I was just going to say no. But Jack's agent sweetened the deal. First I would train Jack to keep his balance on a board and maybe drop into a half-pipe. Then, once the movie started shooting, I would be his stunt double. There was no way I could say no to that. It was the kind of gig that could launch my career.

I have a handshake contract with Jack's agent, which is, apparently, as good as gold. But I would have taken the job for next to nothing. I'm seventeen, and most of my friends are leaving for college in a few weeks. I'm not sure what I want to do with my life, so I'm taking a year off to think about it. A career in skateboarding would be awesome, and being a stunt double in a feature film would be an incredible start.

But back to Goat. Apparently he'd been looking to challenge me to a S.K.A.T.E. competition since he had found out I was going to work with Jack. I guess he felt he had something to prove. Goat is a good skater, one of the best in the area, but he had never been picked up by a skate crew or offered a sponsorship.

He had also never been a stunt double in a movie.

"Come on, Head Case," Goat yelled. My name is Casey Finnegan, though Goat has never once called me Casey. It's always Head Case. "Or do you want to bow out now? I mean, that's cool with me. I got plenty of stuff to do with my day."

There was a bit of a breeze coming in off the ocean, bringing the sea smell with it. It was just after three in the afternoon, and the sky was so blue, I could imagine it wrapping right around the Earth.

"Hold on, Goat," I said. I decided to forget about the 720° for the time being and do the 360° heel flip, then throw something down Goat might embarrass himself with.

I dropped in and got as much speed on the down slope as possible. I pumped once across the bottom of the ramp and dug in to launch myself on the other side. I didn't need much air to do the 360° heel flip, but I wanted to show Goat up a little, so I launched as high as I could.

When you're in the air, the board spinning beneath you, it is both awesome and terrifying. You feel as if anything is possible. You also fear you're about to fall and break something. But that's part of the thrill. Tricks happen in an instant, so there's not much time to think about what you're doing. In fact, thinking usually only gets you into trouble.

I landed on the vertical part of the ramp, leaning far enough forward to get the speed I would need for my next trick. I was tightly coiled, ready to explode, when I hit the other side. As my front wheels came up to the coping, I pushed on my back foot, brought the board up, then launched. I grabbed the nose of my board, took my feet off and managed to get three full swipes in the air to perform an airwalk. After the airwalk, I put the board back under my feet and landed fakie on the vert. As I came up the other side, I did a fakie backside grab, before finally shooting up and hopping off onto the deck.

There were some claps and hoots from the crowd. More people were hanging around today than normal. Word of Jack Coagen's presence must have spread beyond the skate community. Goat stared at me from the other side of the ramp, his long dreads whipping around in the wind. A hush descended on the crowd, and I could hear a camera shutter clicking. Down beside the ramp a tall older guy was taking pictures with the longest camera lens I had ever seen. At first it seemed as if he was taking pictures of me. But then he leaned to one side, and I looked behind me to see

Jack slumped against the railing. Jack didn't even seem to notice the guy. I guess he was used to the attention.

"Your go," I yelled at Goat.

Goat tapped his board on the coping. "My go," he said. "All right, Head Case. All right. If you want to play it like that."

chapter two

Goat planted his back foot down hard on the tail of his board and dropped in. He pumped once across the flat and launched himself three feet above the coping. He only did one kick, which, I guess, is enough to call it an airwalk. He landed with a little tap on the coping that sent him wobbling. But he managed to right himself, launch off the other side and kick out a nice fakie pop shove-it.

"Whoa, Head Case," he said once he had landed on the deck beside me. "Did you see that? Old Goat's learned a new trick."

"Amazing, Goat. I guess what they say about practice is true." I figured it was time for the 720° melon because, even if he had been working on it, I knew Goat couldn't pull it off with ease.

Somebody switched on the big boom box. The Red Hot Chili Peppers' "Higher Ground" bounced off the ramp. I dropped in, pumped across the flat and launched off the coping, floating just high enough to pull off a sketchy pop shove-it. I didn't land quite right and lost all my speed. I had to think fast. The 720° wasn't going to happen. I no longer had the speed or the correct angle. I hit the coping on the other side and launched into a 360° cannonball. A 360° cannonball is a full rotation in the air while holding the front and back of the board. I was fully around the 180° when I thought of something I shouldn't have.

What if I didn't land this?

What if I caught my front trucks on the coping, fell and broke something? I would lose the stunt-double job. And I would lose my shot at making it. For what? To show up a local I had skated with dozens of times?

So I bailed, sliding to the bottom of the ramp with my board spinning and tumbling behind me.

A collective *oooohhhhh* sprang from the deck and the area around the ramp.

Goat didn't even wait until I was off the ramp before he dropped in and threw down a perfect pop shove-it. "T!" he yelled. "Give the man a T!"

The small crew that had come across town with him banged their boards against the coping. The Chili Peppers' "Knock Me Down" belted out as I ran up the ramp. We had decided earlier that whenever someone got a letter, it was the other guy's opportunity to start again with whatever trick he wanted.

Goat was standing on the deck, rubbing his chin as though he was about to come up with a solution to tackle global warming or cure cancer. He raised a finger to the sky and shook it a few times. "Watch this, Jack Coagen," he said, and dropped in.

He skated slowly, did a quick blunt to fakie on the coping, rolled across the flat and back up the other side. There was a collective moan. He had already pulled this move earlier, and it was obvious why he was doing it again. A blunt to fakie, which is when you hit the coping and stop before dropping back into the pipe backward, absolutely kills your speed. You have to pump like hell in order to gain enough speed to hit the coping on the other side, never mind launch. There was no way to do anything other than a simple 180° after a blunt to fakie.

I had to though. I had to figure out something to do on the other wall. Something big.

I dropped in, did the blunt to fakie, spun around on the flat, then shot up the other wall. I didn't have much speed when I hit the coping, so I popped my front foot off, slammed it down and launched into the air. Once I was airborne, I grabbed the front of the board and put my feet on the tail, doing an abrupt but clean rocket air. As I slid my foot back to the front of the board, I turned quickly so I wouldn't land backward. I came smoothly down on the vert before powersliding to a stop on the flat.

"A no comply!" Goat yelled. "Is that the best you can do?"

"It was a no comply to a 180° rocket air, Goat."

"Yeah, yeah." He shook his head as though all of this was suddenly beneath him.

I wasn't sure if he could do a no comply. I had never seen him do one before. But I spent as little time with Goat as possible.

He dropped in, shot up the far wall and took his front foot off the board too late. He missed the coping and was suspended in the air for a moment before his board kicked out from beneath him. For some reason, he leaned forward. Unfortunately, the board landed tail down on the deck and stuck straight up. When gravity got ahold of Goat, his face was the first thing to come in contact with the tip of the board. There was a flash of blood, and he crumpled to one side before sliding down the ramp.

I was the first to reach him. He looked groggy, but I didn't think he had lost consciousness. His nose was bleeding heavily, leaving a big red puddle on the ramp.

"You all right, Goat?" I asked. He looked up at me. I swear his eyes were spinning in his head.

"Just do it," he said, spitting out some blood.

"Do what?"

"The trick. Give me the E." He looked like he wanted to say more, but his brain had been banged around.

"No worries, Goat. We can call it even."

One of Goat's friends pulled him to his feet. "Do it, man. Finish the stupid game," Goat said. He looked as if he was going to swing his skateboard at me.

I clambered up the wall, dropped in, shot past the crowd that had formed on the flat, did as unimpressive a no comply to 180° rocket air as possible, landed and steered off the ramp.

Goat's friends had circled him and were giving me evil glares as they helped him off the ramp. When they walked past me, Goat stopped. He gingerly touched his nose and said, "Next time we play S.K.A.T.E. in a street park." He spit more blood on the ground and turned to walk back to his car. He got about two steps before he was engulfed by a crowd of girls. They all had pieces of paper and Sharpies in their hands, as well as a look in their eyes as if someone was handing out free puppies. Goat looked confused as he pushed through them. I turned around to find Jack behind me, and it suddenly made sense.

Jack's floppy hair blew in the breeze. His eyes were hidden behind huge aviator glasses, but their deep blueness was legendary. He took a piece of paper from one of the girls and quickly scribbled his signature on it. "Not bad," he said to me.

I shrugged. "Thanks."

"Do you think you can teach me how to do all that in two weeks?"

"I could probably get you to the point where you can drop in without breaking anything," I said.

He laughed. "Cool. I'll have you to do the stunt-double work for the rest, right?"

"Exactly," I said.

He took another piece of paper from a girl, scribbled on it and handed it back. "Listen," Jack said, looking over at me as a girl handed him her backpack to sign. "I have to go meet some people." He nodded to the girl when she thanked him and said how much she loved his movies. He scribbled across another piece of paper before holding his hand up. "Sorry, everyone. I have to get going." There was a collective moan. He stepped in front of me and pushed his sunglasses up on his head. "But I want to have a chat," he said. "Can we meet up later?"

"Sure," I said. "Just give me a call." He shook my hand and pushed through the crowd to his car. Everyone watched him go. Once he pulled away, the park filled with sighs and "Oh my gods" and "He's soooo cute."

I wasn't sure what to think of Jack Coagen. I had seen him act in one film and had not been impressed. But I wasn't a thirteen-year-old girl. He seemed nice enough, but you never know. His job, after all, was to pretend to be someone he wasn't. I reminded myself that working with Jack Coagen was an opportunity to make money skateboarding. I couldn't think of anything better, or anything I wanted more.

chapter three

I didn't hear from Jack until ten o'clock that night. I had given up on him and was heading out the door when he finally called. I decided to keep him waiting and went to pick up my friend, Sara Finlay, first. Sara is the best female skater in town. Actually, she's one of the best skaters in town, period. We had been hanging out together for the past year, mostly at the half-pipe. Tonight, though, she had asked if she could come to the beach bonfire with me. Most of my other friends were out of town, looking at apartments or moving into college residences. This was likely to be one of the final beach parties of the year.

"Sorry about leaving today," Jack said, when we picked him up at his hotel.

"That's all right," I said. "It was kind of hectic anyway."

Jack was staying at the new Sheridan. I could remember a time when there was only one hotel in town, a mom-and-pop place off the highway called The Dolphin. But over the years, as people inland and farther up the coast moved toward the sunshine and sea, my little town became a mid-sized city. Which, in a lot of ways, was all right. At least we now have a big movie theater complex, more than one mall and, most importantly, a full-sized skate park.

During the summer, the cottages and oceanfront hotels are packed with people who come to spend their holidays on sunny beaches. But while the summers are hot, the winters are cool. It gets cold enough to clear the town of summer vacationers.

Jack settled into the backseat of my bright red VW Jetta. He looked around at the messy interior as if he had somehow landed on the moon. "Don't get me wrong. I appreciate my fans," he said. "I just get tired of signing my name all the time. I can only take so much of it."

"Yeah," I said. "I bet."

Sara spun around in her seat and introduced herself. "I won't ask for your autograph," she said.

"You don't like my movies?" Jack said with a smirk.

Sara glanced at me, then back at Jack. "I've never actually seen one," she said. "Don't be offended or anything. I don't watch many movies."

Jack shrugged. "No offense taken."

I looked in the rearview mirror. Jack was stretched out on the backseat as though he owned it. He flipped his hand in front of him in a dismissive manner. "I'm done with kid movies anyway," he said.

"It's time to move to the big time. Can't be a kid forever, right?"

"Right," I said.

The flicker of the bonfire's flames was visible in the distance. Open fires on any of the nearby beaches are banned, so normally, beach parties are low-key. If the police find out about them, they rush in and grab whoever they can for underage drinking, public disturbance or whatever other charges they feel like laying.

The Killers' "All These Things I've Done" was playing on someone's iPod speakers near the fire. Its thumping bass line grew louder as we approached. About fifty people gathered around the fire on lawn chairs or leaned against logs.

There was ample booze around, but I don't drink. There's no deep dark reason behind it. I simply don't like the way it makes me feel.

Sean Ragnitz and his buddy Jaden Lairson were set up in lawn chairs, with a cooler between them, selling single bottles of Budweiser to underage drinkers. Everyone pretended to enjoy drinking. Soon enough, though, the alcohol would begin to affect them, and moods would swing unpredictably. Which was always an indication it was time to go.

"Case!" I turned to find Ian Holmes waving at me from his perch on a log. He was about five feet from the fire, and his pale face glowed.

"What's up, Ian?" I said. The three of us walked over to his perch.

"Drink?" he said, raising a bottle.

"Nah, I'm good," I said.

"Yo, I hear you brought out the worst in Goat today." Ian was one of those people who always knew what was going on. He was a hub of information and rumor.

"He bailed, that's all," I said.

"Any hard feelings there?" he asked.

I shook my head. "Why?"

"Because he's over there, and he's been asking about you."

I looked across the fire and spotted Goat standing with his back to me. He was with the rest of his crew, passing a bottle around. Their voices were louder than necessary, and apparently everything they said was the funniest joke ever.

"How long have they been drinking?" I asked. I felt a little shiver down my spine.

"They were here before the fire got lit, man. I think they were here before the sun went down."

"It was a game of S.K.A.T.E.," I said.

Ian nodded. "Good, good." He gave my leg a tap with his fist. "Goat didn't sound hostile or anything. But, you know, if something riles up, I'm here for you, man."

And he would be. Ian was the kind of guy that would always have your back.

"Cool," I said. It was well past the time a party this size was going to remain a secret. Someone turned up the music, and Jack Johnson's "If I Had Eyes" rolled out over the sand.

chapter four

We found some space on a log and sat down to enjoy the party while it lasted. Three senior girls came over and talked to Sara and me, but they all kept glancing at Jack. I introduced everyone. Jack was more interested in the senior girls than he had been with the tweeners at the half-pipe earlier, and I could see why. Megan Paterson, Nichole McGill, Rebecca Vlas–they were all major hotties.

I was talking with Rebecca when Danny McNaughton stepped in front of us and spit on the ground. I looked at his giant bare arms. I had only ever seen McNaughton in something other than long shorts and a white undershirt once, at a funeral for a classmate who died in a Sea-Doo accident.

"What's going on over here?" McNaughton said, resting a hand on Rebecca's shoulder. She cringed and shifted away. He looked down at Jack. "Oh, Teen Beat is here. That's what all the commotion's about. How's it going, Teen Beat?"

"Do I know you?" Jack said.

"This is Danny McNaughton," I said. Rebecca managed to duck under McNaughton's arm and disappear into the crowd.

"That's Mr. McNaughton to you, Finnegan."

"All right," Jack said, before turning back to Megan.

"Yo, Teen Beat," McNaughton said, moving over to introduce Goat. "My friend Fraser, Goat, has something to discuss."

"With you and with Head Case, actually," Goat said, leaning toward us.

McNaughton turned and clapped his hands. "Hey, shut that music down," he yelled. "Everyone, listen up here." The music was silenced and conversations dwindled.

"Jack, I hear you're a decent guy. I'm a decent guy too," Goat said. He had a disgustingly sweet, fake smile on his face. "I want to put a little proposition forward. I know you've hired Head Case to train you in the ways of skateboarding and be your stunt double, but I think you're missing an opportunity here."

"Am I?" Jack asked.

"Your agent, or whoever signed Head Case up, didn't look deeply enough into the local skate community. I would make a better trainer and stunt double. And I can prove it."

"Oh yeah?" Jack said. A little smile had settled on his face. He stood up and brushed sand off his pants. "This sounds interesting. What's your plan?"

Goat turned to me. "You got me today, Head Case. I'll give you that. But overall, I'm a better skater."

"Whatever, Goat," I said, feeling as if everyone was watching us–because everyone was.

"Okay, okay. You might not think so. I can understand that. So here's what I propose. A contest. We'll cover *all* kinds of skateboarding: street, vert, everything. We'll start tomorrow with a street competition. And, to be fair, I say we let Jack be the judge."

Jack was staring at Goat. His eyes narrowed, and he started nodding his head. "That could almost make this place interesting," Jack said. "What do you think, Casey?"

"I think this place is interesting enough as it is," I said.

"Yeah, but it couldn't hurt, could it?" Jack put his hand on my shoulder. "I could learn a lot from watching you guys. Plus, this town is so dead, it needs something to liven it up, or I'm going to die of boredom."

"I think your time would be better spent practicing," I said.

"I only need to learn how to push around a little. Maybe drop in on a ramp. No big deal. What I really need for this part is to *understand* skateboarding."

"I can teach you to drop in and stuff," Goat said. "No problem. But yeah, skateboarding isn't only about pushing around. It's a culture."

"As long as Casey is up to it, I think a contest is a great idea," said Jack. "And nothing with Casey is nailed down yet."

Goat beamed. "What do you say, Head Case?"

I thought it was the dumbest idea I had ever heard. I thought it was stupid and probably dangerous. I also thought there was no way for me to say no. Jack wanted some excitement. If I said no to the contest, he would dump me and hire Goat instead. I was stuck.

"Whatever," I said. "Sure."

"We'll start tomorrow at the skate park over at my end of town. I'll even give you the half-pipe today. You're up one nothing," Goat said. He clapped his hands together and turned back to Jack. "Listen, I noticed the board you had today, and, well, it kinda sucks. Just to show you I'm a decent guy, I brought you this one." He handed a skateboard over to Jack. "It's a little used, but that makes them better."

"Thanks, man," Jack said.

"No problem," Goat said and stepped away from us. "I'll be in touch."

McNaughton leaned forward. "I know you'll make the right decision, Teen Beat." Then, for no other reason than that McNaughton is an asshat, he pushed Jack over a log. Jack toppled backward and fell into Tyler Allen. Now, McNaughton may be big and mean, but he's not unmatched in town.

Tyler cocked his head back and said, "What the hell, McNaughton?"

"My bad," McNaughton said.

"What did you do that for?" I asked.

McNaughton shrugged. "A mistake, that's all. My bad."

Tyler stepped over the log and shoved McNaughton. "Oops," Tyler said. "My mistake. Didn't mean to shove you."

McNaughton shoved him back, and then all hell broke loose. Tyler put his head down, as if he was in the middle of a football game, and tackled McNaughton to the ground. A moment later, two of McNaughton's friends started shoving a couple of Tyler's friends. Jack picked himself up off the sand and ran swinging into the mess of people.

I leaped off the log, pulling Sara with me. People scattered in the jumpy way they do when a fight breaks out. Everyone moved far enough away to not be involved, but not so far they couldn't still watch. I was about to drag Jack out of there, figuring he was partially my responsibility, when a series of bright flashes blinded me.

"What is that light?" Sara said, covering her eyes.

I reached in and grabbed Jack's shoulder. "Come on," I said.

Jack stumbled out of the crowd, and the camera flashes followed him. He swung out at the light, and then he backed away.

I was about to leave him behind when McNaughton tossed Tyler toward us. Jack half caught him and shoved him away. The beach filled with flashlight beams. Everyone started running and yelling, "Cops! Cops!"

"Come on," I said again, grabbing Jack's shirt and pulling him up the bank toward a cluster of trees. We had made it out of the glow of the bonfire when a rush of people came toward us, followed by half a dozen police officers waving flashlights and batons.

"This way," I yelled. I leaped over a log and landed in a marshy area along the edge of the woods. Sara and Jack followed. One cop slowed down as he passed where we had ducked into the trees. But I guess he decided there were already enough kids on the beach to chase after.

I pressed my back against a tree and peered out at the scene on the beach. Sara had fallen into me. I could feel her struggling to catch her breath.

Jack was bent over, heaving in and out, with his hands on knees. "What is that guy's problem?" he said.

"McNaughton or Goat?" I asked.

"The big guy. Does he always shove people around?" Jack asked.

"Yes," I said. Jack looked at me, and I looked away. I was pissed he had put us in this situation and pissed he had gone along with Goat's contest.

"We should get out of here," Jack said. "That paparazzi guy snapped a million pictures. The last thing I need is to get busted and have photos of me being cuffed and dumped in a cruiser." He hefted his new skateboard under his arm.

"So that's what all those flashes were–a camera?" Sara said. "How did he know you were here?"

"They find out." He looked around the wooded area. "How do we get out of here? My shoes are getting ruined in this mud."

I pointed to a path through the woods. "We can get to the road that way, then double back to my car."

Jack started walking without another word.

"Real piece of work, isn't he?" Sara said quietly.

I looked ahead at Jack, and I had to agree with her.

chapter five

The next day it seemed as if the whole town was at the skate park. Normally there would be fifteen or twenty kids taking turns hitting the rails or messing around in the bowls. But today there had to be fifty or sixty people in attendance, many without skateboards.

"Wow, lots of people here today," Sara said as I pulled into the parking lot. This park was on the other end of town from where we lived, and most of the people who rode here went to a different high school.

Goat was leaning against Jack's late-model Lexus. He had chopped his dreads off and was sporting the same kind of floppy hairdo Jack had. He looked strange. His face was rounder than I had thought, and his eyes seemed smaller. He held up his wrist and tapped his watch. "Bit late, Head Case," he said, so everyone could hear.

Jack popped out of his car and shut the door. His hair was spiked up in a faux hawk, and he had those giant sunglasses on again. I don't know if he thought he was getting into the skater culture or what. But he looked ridiculous. "Hey, Casey," he said when Sara and I walked up to his car.

"Hey," I said.

Goat dropped his board and started popping it up and down with his foot. "We going to get this going or what?"

"Someone trick you into going to a barbershop?" Sara said. "What did they do, promise you candy?"

"Ha ha," Goat said. "This girl is a riot." He waved her away and turned to me. "Let's flip to see who goes first." Goat pulled out a coin, and I glanced at Jack.

"That all right with you?" I said.

Jack shrugged and looked away. "Sure."

Goat flipped the coin. I called heads, and it landed tails.

"All right," Goat said. "My choice. How about you go first, Head Case. That way I'll know how much effort I should bother putting into this."

"Hopefully your magical skateboarding skills weren't stored in your dreads," Sara said, but Goat ignored her.

"I say we do two-minute runs. Best run wins," Goat said. "Sound good, Jack?" Jack nodded and pushed himself off the side of the car. "So, you watch each of us and then say who you think does better."

"Cool," Jack said. He pointed to a wall in the middle of the park. "I'll sit up there."

The park consisted of two concrete bowls, a series of launch pads, a dozen different rails and a staircase. It was a decent park, even though there were cracks in the concrete and gullies where water pooled after it rained.

Two minutes is a long time in a competition. You have to use it right–knowing, of course, a great trick can be zeroed out by a big bail. But this wasn't a competition in the true sense. There was no scoring at the end of a run. No best two out of three. Just one run and then Jack's decision.

I scanned the park, trying to figure out a good line. This is the mental part of the competition. You have to believe in yourself. Believe in your abilities. I knew, for instance, I could pull a number of tricks into and out of the bowls. I could even use the bowls as a half-pipe and nail my half-pipe tricks without any problems. But that wasn't what this was about. This was supposed to be a street competition, and though Jack didn't know much about skateboarding, he had no doubt watched enough videos to tell the difference between pipe tricks and street tricks. Half-pipe tricks are clean, full of rotations and grabs. Whereas street tricks are something else entirely. When you do street tricks, you have to hit things hard, force your will upon the obstacles. It is almost a different sport.

"Come on, Head Case, you have two minutes once you start," Goat said. "That doesn't mean you have all day to get going."

I walked across the park to the bowl thinking, Try to feel the flow, try to feel the flow. I looked around at the crowd, zeroed in on the course and forgot anyone else was there.

I considered starting with a backside 360° off the far wall, followed by a kick flip on this side, back into the bowl and transfer with a 540° melon into the other bowl. I visualized the entire run. I would have to stop a few times to get to other sections of the park, but that was part of a street competition.

"Whenever you're ready, Head Case," Goat yelled. He had taken up a spot beside Jack on the wall.

I didn't bother to reply. I pushed down hard on the front of my board and dropped into the bowl. I managed to pull a clean backside 360° off the lip. Then I did a kick flip on the other side, swooped back into the bowl and launched over the transition into the other bowl.

Transitioning from one bowl to another isn't that difficult, but it looks cool. Especially if you get a lot of air, which I did. I landed with the slightest wobble, straightened myself and did a truck grind around the edge of the bowl. The park filled with applause. I dropped back in and decided it was time to get out of the bowls before it looked as if I was treating the park as a half-pipe.

I exited the bowl with a giant airwalk, popped off my board and ran up the stairs. I glanced at Goat. He raised his hand and rocked it back and forth in a so-so gesture. At the top of the stairs there was an angled drop-in alongside another set of stairs with a handrail. I pushed hard toward the handrail, ollied at just the right moment and caught the rail about halfway down, sliding along it and landing backward. I spun around and ollied onto a box, kick-flipped off and rolled up a slight incline on the other side.

The crowd was really getting into it. I was feeling the flow now. Everything seemed to be working perfectly. I took my time climbing back up the stairs. I had hit the rail so well that I wanted to try something else on it, maybe a kick flip to tail slide. The problem was, when I reached the top of the stairs, I couldn't decide what would be the most impressive. I dropped my board and pushed toward the stairs. I ollied high enough to reach the rail and tried to kick-flip, but the board caught on the rail and spun away from me. My left foot slid out as I tried to stay upright. There was nothing to hold on to and nowhere to go but down. I crashed onto the stairs, banging my shoulder and shin as I went down. The crowd gasped. A stabbing pain shot up my leg, and everything went black.

chapter six

I shook my head, and the skate park came back into focus. I tried to stand up, but the pain piercing through my shin was so severe, I wasn't able to put any weight on my leg.

"You all right?" Jack yelled.

I raised an arm, and people clapped. I finally stood, favoring my left leg, and retrieved my board. My vision wavered, and I thought I might puke. I dropped my board and pushed toward a little triangle ramp. I tried a 180° ollie. My shin felt as if it would snap in two when I landed, so I stepped off my board, popped it into my hand and raised my other arm to the crowd.

"You still have forty-five seconds," Goat yelled.

"I'm good," I said.

Goat said something to Jack. I couldn't tell whether Jack replied, but I didn't think it mattered. I had bailed big-time. My shin felt as if it was bleeding through my cargo pants, and my shoulder was going to be seriously bruised. As much as I would have loved to keep skating, it wasn't going to happen.

Goat sat on top of the wall, holding his watch in front of him, his new floppy haircut flipping in the breeze. He waited for the full forty-five seconds to pass before he began clapping.

"Time's up," he said as he hopped down from the wall. He walked over to me, wrapped an arm across my shoulders and squeezed. "Nice run, Head Case."

He slapped me on the back and dropped his board. "Just going to get set up here, Jack."

Jack nodded. I considered sitting with him on the wall, but I resented his involvement in this. His agent had contacted me—*me*—to train him and be his stunt double. Whether I had a signed contract or not shouldn't have mattered. I didn't know if Jack was going along with Goat's plan just for the entertainment or not. But there was nothing I could do about it. I went and stood beside Sara.

"You okay?" she asked.

I resisted the urge to lift my pant leg and look at my shin. "Yeah," I said.

Goat was still on the course, rubbing his chin and looking around as if he had never been there before. The park was right behind his house. He spent more time here than anywhere else. Though Jack wouldn't know this.

Goat decided to start with the handrail. He pulled a perfect kick flip to nose slide on the rail. He followed this with a pop shove-it onto the block and a kick flip off.

Everything he did was smooth and fluid and beautiful. He circled around the bowls, dropped in and did a few flip tricks and grinds before running back up the stairs and landing a perfect rail slide. It wasn't two minutes' worth of tricks, but it didn't matter. He had done everything perfectly. And, he hadn't fallen.

He rode over to the wall and looked up at Jack. "What do you say?" he yelled.

Jack slid his sunglasses up on his head and jumped off the wall. I walked over, already certain what the verdict would be.

"I only know so much about skateboarding," Jack said. "Like, from videos and stuff. But you were both really good. I mean, I'd be lucky to have either of you training me. Casey, how you went between the two bowls was wicked. And Goat, the grinds and, what do you call them, flip tricks?"

"Yeah, flip tricks," Goat said. "Those are the technical ones."

"Those were amazing," said Jack. "So in the end, I guess I have to give this one to you, Goat." There was a commotion behind us in the crowd, but Jack didn't seem to notice. "It's because you fell, Casey. I mean, that's pretty much all it comes down to."

"Sure," I said, looking over at the crowd.

"But it's not the end, right?" Jack said. "We're going to–"

Two police officers appeared behind us, and a kid I didn't recognize pointed at Jack.

"Jack Coagen?" one of the officers said.

Jack turned around. "Yeah?"

"We'd like you to come with us," said the officer. "We have a few questions about an incident last night."

"What?" Jack said, slipping his sunglasses back over his eyes.

The officer flashed Jack an insincere smile. "We'd rather not discuss this here," he said.

"Am I under arrest for something?" Jack asked.

I was amazed at how he was talking to the police. If it had been me, I would have said, "All right," and gone with them.

"We need to have a little conversation about an incident," the officer repeated more slowly.

Jack crossed his arms in front of his chest. "Am. I. Under. Arrest?" Jack asked again.

The second officer shook his head and stepped away, pulling a two-way radio off his belt. The crowd parted again, and the photographer who had been at the half-pipe and the beach party the day before appeared and started snapping photos.

"No, you're not under arrest," the first officer said. He was a big guy with the kind of red ruddy cheeks people get from being outside a lot. He had one hand on his belt.

"Well, I'm not going anywhere. And I'm not really interested in answering any questions," Jack said. The photographer kept taking photos, shooting them off one after another. Jack turned his back to the photographer, but it didn't seem to dissuade him. "Not until you tell me what this is all about."

"Fine," the first officer said. "There are accusations you either intentionally or accidently injured a girl at an illegal beach party at Heath's Head last night."

"What?" Jack said. "Who?"

"We are not at liberty to disclose the individual's identity," said the officer. "Were you at Heath's Head last night?"

"Yeah. But I didn't hurt anyone," Jack said.

The second officer slid the two-way radio back into his belt and came over. He pointed at a cruiser in the parking lot. "Could you turn this way for us?" the first officer said to Jack.

"What?" Jack said. "No, I didn't–"

The first officer grabbed Jack's arm and spun him around. The photographer went wild and shot off dozens of photos. "Look toward the police car, son," the first officer said, sounding tired with the whole thing. The second officer pulled his radio from his belt again and held it to his ear.

"Get your hands off me," Jack said, shaking the first officer's hand off his arm. "You can't do that."

"Look toward the car, please," the first officer repeated.

Jack stood still. He looked at the cruiser's darkened windows.

The second officer stepped away. He strapped the radio back onto his belt and said, "She says it's not him."

"Who says it's not me?" Jack said. "What's going on here?"

"It's been cleared up," the second officer said. "Sorry to bother you."

"Sorry to bother me?" Jack said.

"Sure," the first officer said. "Sorry to bother you." And without another word, the two of them walked back to their car.

"What was that all about?" Goat asked.

"I don't know," Jack said. "But I'm going to call my agent about it." He jammed his hands into his pockets and kicked his skateboard into the wall. When it rolled back to him, he picked it up and gripped it tightly. He kept an eye on the photographer. "What's up next?" he said through clenched teeth.

Goat looked at me. "Any ideas?"

My leg hurt too much to care. Whatever part of the contest was going to happen next would have to wait for another day. "No."

"Well, I have one," Goat said.

"Okay. What is it?" I asked.

Goat looked around the park. A couple of skaters had dropped into the course, and the *tap tap tap* of skateboard tails bouncing off concrete started up. "I can't say right now," he said. "How about..." Goat stopped. A couple of people milling around behind us were leaning forward, trying to eavesdrop. Goat put his arms around Jack and me and pulled us close. "How about we meet at the parking lot down at the beach? Say tonight at nine?"

"Sure," Jack said, pulling his phone out of his pocket. "I'll be there." Then he walked back to his car, his phone stuck to his ear.

"What do you have in mind, Goat?" I asked.

He smiled and gave me a shot in the shoulder. "You'll see, Head Case. You'll see."

chapter seven

The beach parking lot was eerily quiet for a Saturday evening. Sara and I were sitting on a picnic table, watching the tide roll in, when the headlights from Goat's piece-of-junk Honda approached.

"What do you think he has planned?" Sara asked.

"I have no idea," I said.

"How's your leg?"

"It still hurts, but I'll be all right," I said, though it wasn't the truth. My shin felt five times larger than normal. I cringed every time I put weight on that leg. But I would have to suck it up.

"You know, you don't have to do any of this," Sara said as we watched Goat get out of his car. The windows were tinted, so it was a surprise when Danny McNaughton swung out of the passenger's side.

"Yes, I do," I said. "If I don't, where'll I be?"

"Right where you were last week, before Jack's agent contacted you," she said. "Life wasn't so bad way back then, was it?"

"No," I said. "But it could be better."

"Your call."

Goat and McNaughton crossed the parking lot and stood before us in the sand. "Where's Jack?" Goat asked.

"Playing hide-and-seek," Sara said. "Your turn to go find him."

"Ha ha," Goat said. He looked at McNaughton. "She's a funny girl. What do you think, Danny? Is she a funny girl?"

"A riot," McNaughton said.

"What are you doing here?" I asked McNaughton.

"He wants to apologize to Jack for what happened last night at the beach," Goat said. Yeah right, I thought, of course he does.

"Listen, Head Case, no hard feelings about all this, right? I just figured–"

"I know what you figured, Goat," I said, cutting him off. I didn't want to hear anything from Goat. He shrugged and turned to look up the road. We waited in silence for another minute or so before Jack's Lexus pulled up behind us. He got out of the car with his phone to his ear and absently dropped the skateboard Goat had given him on the ground.

"Hey, Jack, glad you could–" Goat stopped when Jack raised a finger.

Jack leaned against his car and stared out at the ocean as he continued talking on his phone. Finally he finished his conversation, grabbed his board, slapped on a big smile and walked over to the picnic table.

"Sorry about that," he said. "Business." He looked at McNaughton. "What are you doing here? Looking to shove people around again?"

"I came to say I'm sorry 'bout that," McNaughton said.

"Really?" Jack said.

"I get kinda crazy sometimes. No offense." McNaughton stuck his hand out. "Friends?"

Jack stared at McNaughton for a moment, and then he shook his hand. "Next time a gentle tap on the shoulder would do, huh?" Jack said. "And no more of that 'Teen Beat' stuff either."

"Sure, sure," McNaughton said.

Jack turned to me. "So, what's on for tonight?"

"I have no idea. Goat's the one who called us here," I said.

"Right. Okay. So," Goat said, "you want to learn about true skate culture, right?"

"Sure," Jack said, not sounding all that enthusiastic.

"Well, skating is a large part of it," said Goat. "Another part, a part I'd say is just as important, is the danger of skating forbidden places."

"Forbidden places?" Jack asked.

"Yeah. I mean, people have hated skateboarders since the seventies," said Goat. "We're banned from streets and sidewalks and malls."

"Okay, so where are we going tonight?" Jack asked.

"Henderson's pool," Goat said. I felt Sara tense up beside me.

"And what is Henderson's pool?" Jack asked.

"Simply the cleanest, purest, most empty pool in town. It's in this dude's backyard. And it is huge. Something like ten feet deep. There's also a hot tub and a shallow area. It is absolutely perfect."

"And empty in August?" Jack asked.

"Empty all the time," Goat said. "It's been empty for five years. But here's the amazing thing: it is still cleaned weekly."

"What?" Jack said. "Why?"

"Because Henderson's wife died in it," I said. "Which is also why Mr. Henderson would lose his mind if he caught anyone skating it."

"Someone died in the pool?" Jack asked. He seemed more curious than freaked-out.

"Yeah," Goat said. "Mrs. Henderson. Rumor has it she was drunk, fell in and drowned. Since then Henderson has kept the pool empty and perfectly clean."

"And you want to skate this place?" Jack asked.

"No," I said.

"You don't have to, Head Case," Goat said. "But this is all part of it, Jack. All part of the real skater attitude. Isn't this the kind of thing you need so you can get into your character?"

"I don't know," Jack said. "Seems like it might be a sacred place."

"It's a pool," Goat said. "A beautiful, clean, perfect pool."

Jack shrugged. "All right, I'll come watch. I mean, I wouldn't be able to skate it, would I?"

"I doubt it," Goat said. "It's a steep drop-in. But give me a week. I could train you to, no problem."

"What about you, Casey?" Jack asked.

I stared at Goat. He had me cornered, and we both knew it. If I backed out, that would be the end of it. Jack would hire Goat to train him. But there was something about Henderson's pool. Something, as Jack said, that was sacred. It didn't feel right. Never mind that we might get caught. "I don't know," I said.

"I have it on good authority that Mr. Henderson is out of town at the moment," Goat said.

"You do, do you?" Sara said. "What authority is that? Did your pet hamster tell you?" She turned to me. "Come on, Casey, this is stupid."

"How would Jack judge who is best?" I asked.

"I don't know. How about you decide, Head Case," said Goat.

I thought about it for a moment. I didn't have many options. "We drop in at the same time," I said. "First one to bail loses."

"Sounds good," Goat said. He looked to Jack. "Sound all right to you?"

"Sure," said Jack.

"No contact," I said. "No cutting the other guy off. Nothing but skating. No stopping. No rolling around in the bottom of the pool. You have to hit one side, then the other, and go full-out."

"Head Case," Goat said. "When have I ever *not* gone full-out? Come on, let's go before it's past your bedtime. We can take my car."

chapter eight

The Henderson house was at the bottom of a road that passed through a section of forest and ended at the ocean. There were no other houses in the area. Goat pulled up to the curb and parked as far away as he could from the only streetlight on the block. We all grabbed our boards and climbed out of Goat's car.

"This is the only way in," Goat said.

It was dark and cool as we stepped from the street into the forest. We hiked up an incline, pushing our way through branches and bushes until we came to a chain-link fence. It was true: to a skater, Henderson's pool was a beautiful thing.

"His backyard is gated, so we have to climb the fence," said Goat.

I could hear the waves washing against the shore and the caw of seagulls circling overhead.

"I'd rather not," Jack said. He had his skateboard with him, but we all knew he wouldn't be riding the pool.

"That's cool. You can stay out here," Goat said.

"What about you?" I asked Sara.

"Whatever," she said. I knew she would love to skate Henderson's pool. I also knew she would never do it–not because she was scared of getting caught, but because she felt it was wrong.

"I'm going to go wait in the car," McNaughton said. He and Goat had been friends since they were kids, but McNaughton was more interested in football than skateboarding. We'd probably return to find him half-asleep in Goat's car, listening to a country singer moan about a broken truck and a dead dog.

"Do you want to climb over?" I asked Sara.

She narrowed her eyes. "No, I can watch you be an idiot just as easily from here. I'll stay with Jack."

"Perfect," Goat said. He put one foot through a link in the fence, pulled himself up and threw his board over the top. I did the same. The two of us climbed the fence and dropped over the other side.

My shin screamed when I landed on the hard concrete surrounding the pool. I grabbed my leg and looked up to find Goat smiling at me.

"A bit tender, Head Case?" he asked.

"I'll be fine," I said. I stepped forward to retrieve my board, and the pool exploded with light.

"Don't worry about it. Old man Henderson ain't around," said Goat. He grabbed his board and looked at the pool. "That is beautiful." He turned to me.

"Let's say we roll in, all right? Take it easy to start off?" He glanced at my shin.

"Sure."

Goat squinted into the darkness back toward where Jack and Sara were. "One of us bails, and it's over, cool?"

"Cool," Jack said.

Goat and I walked to the edge of the shallow end and stepped in. The pool gradually got deeper until it was a full ten feet deep. It was shaped like a keyhole, perfectly round at the deep end, and straight and square at the shallow end.

Goat dropped his board. "On the count of three," he said.

I dropped my board and put my foot on the tail. "One, two, three."

We both pushed a few times and crouched, skating in opposite directions of the deep end. Neither of us hit the lip of the pool the first time. We cruised and dropped back in. The surface was so clean and smooth, we barely made any noise.

I cut around Goat as we both reached the bottom of the pool and shot up the other side. I had gained enough speed to do a quick front side grab near the lip. It felt amazing. So amazing, I almost forgot I was competing.

There was a lot of room in the pool, but every time we reached the bottom, Goat and I had to cross paths. I wouldn't say he was trying to hit me, but he wasn't working very hard to get out of the way either.

"Watch yourself, Head Case," Goat said. "You look wobbly." He did a little tail tap on the edge of the pool, dropped back in and cruised around the side. I cut beneath him and launched off the other side to do a simple backside 180°.

We had been in the pool for a minute or so, which doesn't sound long, but when you're pumping and bending and straining to stay on a board, it feels like an eternity.

"Maybe we should liven this up a little," Goat said as he shot past me.

"How so?"

"True old-school death match."

"What?" I said as we passed each other again.

"Anything goes. Cut the other guy off. Slam into him. Shove him. Whatever."

"No, forget it," I yelled back. I cut up to the shallow end of the pool and rolled around for a second to catch my breath.

"Why not? What are you afraid of?"

I rolled over to the edge of the deep end and dropped in. "Nothing," I shouted. "But it's not what we agreed to."

"So," Goat said, cutting very close. "Rules can change."

Goat had a good fifteen pounds on me. Plus he was taller, which gave him a much longer reach. We both knew if it came to a death match, he would win. The only chance I had of winning was if we kept skating. He was getting tired, and I had seen him catch the edge of the pool a couple of times.

"We can't stay in here forever," Goat said as he swept into the shallow end and made the same half circle I had.

"I got all night," I said. He dropped back into the deep end and tucked straight toward me. I swerved at the last second and wobbled slightly going up the wall. "Goat, forget it. We agreed to—"

Goat did a quick turn on the far wall and was coming straight at me again. "Forget whatever we agreed to," he said. "I'm tired of this."

I managed to cut around him and back into the pool. I was going way too fast, and suddenly, I was high along the edge. Goat came in beneath me, making it impossible to drop back in. I did a power-slide, and Goat shot around to the other side of the pool. I dropped back in, tucked up the ramp to the shallow end, making sure I didn't put a foot down. Goat came up behind me. As I turned to go back into the deep end, he reached out and tried to shove me. I ducked and rolled into the deep end.

I was about to shoot up the wall, figuring I didn't have any other option but to gun it straight for him, when a bright spotlight lit up the lawn and someone yelled, "What the hell is going on out here?"

chapter nine

I skidded to a stop and drifted down to the bottom of the pool. A man stood near the edge of the shallow end with something in his hand. "What do you think you're doing in there?" he said.

Goat tucked down the incline toward the deep end, rocketed up the opposite wall, clambered out of the pool and beelined for the fence.

"There's two of them in my pool," I heard the man say. He had a cordless phone in his hand. "Hey, get back here, you!"

Goat had made it over the fence and was on the other side.

"Come on out of there," the man said. "I've called the police. They'll be here in a minute. You can tell them who your friend is that just took off."

I had to think fast. I couldn't climb out of the deep end of the pool. There wasn't a ladder, and the sides were slick and smooth. I started walking toward the shallow end, my head down and my hoodie pulled low over my face.

"This is private property," he said. "Why would you do this?"

I wanted to tell him I was sorry. That it wasn't my idea. But what would he care? And it didn't matter anyway. My idea or not, I had agreed to go along with this.

I walked about three-quarters of the way up the incline. Then I dropped my board and pushed as hard as I could back into the deep end.

"Hey!" he yelled. Somehow I had enough speed to reach the lip of the pool. I rolled over the top and onto the concrete that circled the pool.

"Get back here," the man yelled. He was making his way toward the deep end. He had a fuzzy housecoat and slippers on. One of his slippers fell off, and he turned to retrieve it.

I ran for the fence, my shin aching, and tossed my board over. I was halfway up before he reached me. He grabbed my foot and tried to pull me down. I held on tight and kicked him with my other foot. He yelped and grabbed his hand, freeing me to pull myself over the fence. I landed on the other side with a smack, picked my board up and hobbled toward the forest, my leg feeling worse than ever.

"You think this is funny?" he said. "Ruining people's property? You think it's a game? You kids have no respect. None at all."

I cut through the bushes back toward the road, where I hoped Sara and Jack were waiting.

"You'll get yours," the man yelled. "The police are on their way. When they ask me if I want to press charges, the answer will be yes. Do you hear me!"

Branches whipped at my face as I ran through the darkness. I heard noises coming from the street. It sounded like a car revving up and down. I headed toward it and slowed down at the edge of the woods.

Jack was standing in the middle of the street beside Goat's old Honda.

McNaughton stuck his head out the driver's-side window. "Get in," he said. Jack moved to open the door, but McNaughton mashed the gas, lurched forward and then stopped.

"Come on, McNaughton," Jack yelled. "Let me in."

McNaughton revved the engine. "All right, come on, hurry up before the cops show."

Jack walked toward the car. Just as his hand touched the door handle, the car shot forward again.

I heard a "pssst" behind me. I squinted into the darkness and saw Sara waving at me, her back pressed against a tree.

"What's going on?" I asked.

"McNaughton," Sara said. "The one and only."

"What a jerk."

"On the plus side, if the cops do show, we're here and they're out there being idiots."

McNaughton gunned the car again. I could hear Goat say something to him from the passenger seat. "Forget it, Goat," McNaughton yelled. "Let him walk." McNaughton must have nailed the gas, because the car fishtailed away, leaving Jack in the middle of the road.

"Jack," I yelled. "Over here." He ran toward my voice. "Hurry up. Henderson called the cops."

Jack ducked into the brush and knelt beside us. We were only half a block from Henderson's house. But to walk on the road would be advertising our guilt. I wished we hadn't all come in one car.

A police cruiser shot past, its lights and siren off. We watched it pull up in front of Henderson's and waited to hear the doors open and close.

"When they go inside to talk to him, we run," I said. "Don't get on your boards until we're a long way from here."

"All right," Sara said.

"Why don't we stay in the woods?" Jack said. "We could try to find a path to the beach."

I grabbed his shoulder. "Maybe. But that's a long walk through the woods at night. And I have no idea where we would come out. No, it's safer to stay on the road."

The officers were still sitting in their cruiser. The interior light was on, and one of them was typing on a laptop. When they got out, they shone their flashlights across Henderson's front lawn and the adjoining woods.

"Wait," I said. The officers clicked their flashlights off and walked to the front door. "Okay, let's go." We were about to dart onto the sidewalk when a gray Toyota rolled up in front of our hiding spot. We pulled back into the bushes and crouched as close to the ground as possible. The driver had a digital device of some kind in his hand. He stopped the car and opened his door. When he stepped out, I recognized him as the photographer that kept snapping shots of Jack everywhere.

"How did he find us here?" I whispered.

"I don't know," Jack said. "Maybe he listens to the police scanners."

"What's in his hand?" Sara asked.

The photographer kept looking at the device and then up at the darkened forest. He took a couple of steps forward, noticed the police cruiser down the street, got back in his car and drove off.

"Let's get out of here," Jack said.

"Yeah," I said. "Let's go." As we walked quickly down the street, I tried to forget how angry, and sad, Mr. Henderson had looked. I tried to focus on why I was doing all this. But most of all, I wanted to know how that photographer had found us.

chapter ten

The next day, when Sara and I arrived at the half-pipe, my leg was still hurting. I sat on the ramp and watched Sara pull off some beautiful airs. We had plans to meet Jack here, but, as always, he was late. It was a warm, late-August Sunday, and it seemed as if everyone in town who skated was at the ramp or messing around on a few street obstacles set up on the basketball court.

Sara rolled to the top of the ramp and hopped off. Someone else dropped in, and the steady drone of wheels on plywood started up again.

"That was really good," I said.

"Could be better," she said. "I'm tired today. Out too late, you know?" She leaned against the back railing and slid down beside me. She didn't say anything for a minute. Then she said, "Casey, why are you doing this?" Which was exactly what I had been thinking,

"Doing what?" I said.

"The stupid competition with Goat that Jack is making you do."

"Because I don't have a choice, Sara. I told you that before."

"You always have a choice. You can say no."

"And then Goat gets the trainer and stunt-double work? Did you see how he's already cut his hair so he looks more like Jack?"

"So what, Casey. I mean, what do you need to be a stunt double for?"

"To make money. To have a career. To do what I love."

"You can skate whenever you want. You don't have to be a stunt double to do that. You're seventeen! Why are you even thinking about a career?"

I shook my head. "Sure, I can skate all I want, but the days will tick away. I have to find something to do," I said.

She crossed her arms in front of her. "You're good in school when you work at it. You're smart. You can go to college." Sara was going to college, and one of her few deficiencies was that she could not understand why anyone else *wouldn't*. "It seems stupid. Jack's playing games with you guys, and he's loving it. He has all this power."

"No, he doesn't," I said quickly.

Sara shrugged and stood up. "Whatever you say, Casey." She put the tail of her board on the coping and dropped back in.

Jack arrived an hour late. He got out of his car with his cell phone to his ear. He was in a real skater outfit today. Someone had probably shipped the clothes to him, and he had put them on without a thought, in anticipation of the paparazzi. Sara was right. Jack was playing a game. He was playing a game with Goat and me, and he was playing a game with himself. It was a game called Pretend. After all, that's where movie stars live, in a pretend world. He needed this new skater image to help him move beyond his kid-actor status. And he was doing everything he could to get there.

Jack dropped his phone in a pocket, grabbed his skateboard out of the trunk and ran up the ramp. "How's it going, Casey?" he said.

"All right," I said. I had a flashback of Jack trying to get in Goat's car, McNaughton driving away and Jack's humiliation.

"Where's Goat?" asked Jack.

"I haven't seen him since last night, when he tried to knock me off my board, ran away and left us stuck on the side of the road."

Jack shrugged. "It's all part of it, isn't it?" he asked.

I frowned. "Getting ditched and left for the police? What is that part of?"

"The culture, man," Jack said. "I mean, that really got my heart pumping." He put his board down and spun it in little circles with his foot. He wasn't going to try and drop in or anything. Being here was all show.

The same gray Toyota from the night before pulled into the parking lot, and the same photographer guy stepped out.

"How does that guy know where you are all the time?" I asked. "Do you tell him or something?"

Jack looked over at the photographer. "Why would I do that?"

"Publicity?"

Jack shook his head. "Man, I'm trying to lay low these days, get ready for my next role, that's all."

"But how does he know where you are all the time?" I asked.

Jack shrugged. "I don't know. He must be lucky."

It didn't sound like a believable explanation to me, but what did I care? It wasn't my face being splashed all over the tabloids.

Goat's crappy Honda pulled into the lot, and as he approached, I noticed something in his hand. He came up to the ramp and waved it at us. "Yo, what's up?" he yelled.

Jack let go of his board. It rolled down the ramp, and he dropped to his knees and slid down after it.

I dropped in, pulled a single excruciating backside air and skated over to see what Goat had planned.

chapter eleven

"What was that all about last night, Goat?" I asked.

"What?" he said.

"Taking off on us."

"That was McNaughton. He was being a jerk. No hard feelings, right?" Goat said.

"Yeah," I said. "Yeah, hard feelings. We could have been busted."

"Did Henderson see you?" Goat asked.

"Not dead on. But my clothes, yeah. He could likely identify me," I said.

Goat waved the thought away. "What are you getting so angry about? Nothing happened. We had a cool time, right, Jack?"

"Yeah," Jack said. "It was intense."

"Where is McNaughton?" I asked. Sara had popped off the ramp and stood beside me.

"He went with his brother down to LA," Goat said.

Of course he did, I thought. He wouldn't want to face us after what he'd done.

"You won't have to worry about him for a week or so," said Goat. He waved the bundle of papers in his hand at us. "Who cares about McNaughton? Do you want to hear my next idea?"

"What next idea?" I asked.

"For the competition. I mean, you won the first one. I nailed the street course, and we have to call last night in the pool a tie," Goat said.

"Why would we call it a tie?" I asked.

"Well, it got interrupted," Goat said.

"That's not the way I see it," I said.

"Okay, how do you see it, Head Case?"

"I saw you jump off your board well before I laid a foot on the ground. I won," I said.

Goat shook his head. "Really? What did you want us to do, keep skating until the police showed? Say, 'Sorry, officer, we'll be right with you, right after we finish this little competition'?"

"If you think it's so stupid, then why are we doing it?" I asked.

Goat sighed and laid the mass of papers against his leg. He turned to Jack. "Would *you* like to hear what I've come up with?"

"Sure, man," Jack said.

"All right, I was reading the script–" said Goat.

"What script?" I said.

Goat turned to me and said very slowly, "The movie script."

I hadn't read a script. I didn't even know there *was* one. "Why do you have it?"

"I asked for it," Goat said. "We need to have competitions that have something to do with the actual film, right? So I figured

I'd read the script and see what whoever becomes the stunt double will have to do."

"You can have a copy as well, Casey," Jack said. "You just never asked. I was telling my agent about Goat, and he had no problem sending a script over. I'm sure he would do the same for you."

Great, I thought. Now Jack's been talking to his agent about Goat. "Sure, send me the script," I said.

"All right, so there's this old-school scene near the end of the script," said Goat. "It's a downhill."

"Yeah," Jack said. "That's a throwback to old skate films. What do you think?"

"I love it," Goat said. "And it got me thinking we should have a competition like that."

"Like what?" I asked.

"A downhill." Goat held the script out. "In here, it says the skaters ride long boards."

"Yeah, that's right," Jack said. "I've never been on a long board."

"They're like normal skateboards, only longer, and the wheels are bigger," I said.

"You can go way faster on them." Goat liked long boards. I could ride one, but they weren't really my thing.

"Is there somewhere around here you guys could do a downhill run on long boards?" Jack asked. He smiled and brushed his floppy hair out of his face.

"Beacon Hill," Goat said.

I shook my head immediately. "No way, Goat."

"What?" Jack said. "What is Beacon Hill?"

"It's this road that's only open in the winter," I said. "It's just for trucks and plows to get up the mountain during ski season."

"A kid died skating down it last year," Sara said. "Skateboarding on it is banned now."

"Sure, sure," Goat said. "Skateboarders are banned from everywhere. Who will know? It's not as if anyone lives on the road or even drives on it."

"How do you get up there?" Jack asked.

"There's another road that cuts across the top of the mountain. You can walk to Beacon Hill from it," I said.

"Is it really that dangerous?" Jack asked.

"Yes," I said.

"It's all right if you know what you're doing," Goat said.

I did not want to ride Beacon Hill. I had heard of skaters going fifty or sixty miles an hour down it. There's no way to control yourself at that kind of speed.

"Well, a stunt like this is going to be in the movie," Jack said.

"Exactly," Goat said.

Jack looked at me. "So, you would have to be able to do it for that, Casey. I mean, if you're going to be my stunt double and all."

"Exactly!" Goat said again.

"What do you think, Casey?" said Jack.

I shook my head. "It's dangerous, Jack. Really dangerous."

"Don't think you can handle it?" Goat said.

"No, I can handle it. It's just..."

"Perfect. All right. How about we meet here tonight," said Goat. "Say around seven? I can drive us to the top of

Beacon Hill, and Jack can leave his car at the bottom."

"Sure," Jack said.

"I'll bring a bike you can ride down behind us," Goat said. "You all right on a bike?"

"Oh yeah," Jack said. "No worries."

No worries, I thought. Yeah, sure. No worries at all.

chapter twelve

"This is the last time I'm going to say it. You don't have to do this," Sara said. We were back at the half-pipe, waiting for Jack and Goat.

"Yes, I do," I said.

"No, you don't, Casey. It's stupid. You could get killed."

"Sara," I said. "I don't have a choice. Now drop it."

Jack's Lexus pulled into the parking lot, followed by Goat's crappy Honda.

Sara was rigid. But I didn't care. I had to put everything out of my mind. I had borrowed a long board from a surfer friend and spent the afternoon practicing on it. Sara had been helping me. But she wasn't what you would call encouraging. She must have told me fifty times that I was going to bust my head open. I couldn't disagree.

"Casey," Jack said as he swung out of his car. "Are you ready for this or what? I am so stoked!"

"Sure," I said. I wished my leg was feeling better. I wished I was more comfortable on a long board. I wished I didn't have to do any of this.

Goat came running up behind Jack. "Everyone ready?" he said.

"Looks like it," Jack said.

Goat looked at Sara. "You won't be able to come," he said. "I have a bike for Jack in my car, so there's no room. You could stay with Jack's car at the bottom of the mountain, if you want."

"That's all right. I wasn't going anyway," she said. She turned around and started toward her house.

"Wait!" I said, chasing after her. She ignored me and kept walking. I grabbed her shoulder, but she shrugged me off. "Sara, wait."

"Why?" she said, turning around. "Are you suddenly going to listen to me and quit this?"

"Sara," I said. "I can't." I could tell she was angry by the way she was standing with her hip jutting out to one side.

She frowned. "Well, I can't watch you." She started walking away again.

"Sara," I said one last time.

"If you survive, give me a call. I'll be at my grandparents for a few days, so..." She stopped and turned to face me. "I don't know. Just call me."

I nodded. There was nothing else to say.

"None of this is worth killing yourself over," she said. She crossed the ramp over to the trail that cut up to her house, and was gone.

"You ready to go?" Goat yelled.

"Yeah," I said. I wanted this over. All of it.

Beacon Hill looked like it went straight down. I'm sure it was some kind of illusion, but standing at the top felt as if we were about to drop into a half-pipe rather than roll down a hill. The road zigzagged toward the bottom of the mountain. On one side of the road was a straight cliff up, and on the other side was a straight cliff down. Everywhere else was trees. The land was too steep to build houses on, so the mountain had been turned into a national conservation area.

"This is really steep, guys," Jack said. It had taken us longer than we had expected to park Jack's car at the bottom and drive up in Goat's Honda. We got lost on one of the trails, which ate up another half hour. It was almost dark by the time we reached the top of Beacon Hill at eight thirty. The sky was purple, and long shadows stretched across the road. A drizzling rain had begun.

It wasn't that bad, but it would soon make the road slick.

"That's the point, Jack," Goat said. He looked up at the sky. "We should get going before it gets any darker or really starts to rain. It should take about twenty minutes to get to the bottom."

"That long?" Jack said.

"It's a long way down," Goat said.

Jack was sitting on an old mountain bike, his arms folded across the handlebars. "And you both think you can do it?" Jack asked.

"I guess we're going to find out," Goat said. "First one down wins. Right?"

Jack shrugged. "I guess that'd be the best way to decide."

"No pushing or cutting off," I said.

"Sure, sure," Goat said. But that's what he had said at the pool as well.

"I'll follow you guys, but I might be a bit behind. I'm not great on a bike," Jack said.

"You'll be fine," Goat said, giving him a pat on the shoulder. "All right, Head Case, you ready?"

I nodded. "On the count of three. One. Two. Three."

I pushed off hard right away. Though I didn't really need to. Beacon Hill was steep. Really steep. After I rounded the first corner, I realized I would have to powerslide to keep my speed down, which was going to become difficult as the pavement got wetter.

Goat and I were neck and neck after the first two corners, but then I did a short powerslide and he shot ahead. I cut to the inside of the road as we neared the next corner, intending to angle myself so that I didn't lose too much speed. Goat didn't think to do the same, and he ended up with two wheels on the road's gravel shoulder. Somehow he managed to get back onto the pavement before he wiped out. He did a couple of long turns to steady himself, and I passed him.

The road seemed as if it was built by someone who'd chased a rabbit down the hill to mark the way. There didn't look as if there was any logic to where the turns were located. But I didn't have much time to think about how the road was constructed. The corners were coming faster and faster. I tried to slow down by powersliding, but I only went faster. I kept an eye on the side of the road, looking for a place to bail if I needed to.

When I hit a rock going around a corner, the back end of my board kicked out. It took everything I had to keep the wheels on the ground and my feet on the deck. I curved straight across the road, leaned hard on the front of my board and cut the other way. I was about halfway across when Goat appeared out of nowhere. I was facing uphill, and he barreled right at me. I dodged him, but as he passed he shot his arm out and clobbered me on the side of the head. I tipped forward and flew off my deck. I hit the pavement hard and slid at least ten feet. My board flipped and slid into the rock face.

Goat looked over his shoulder and laughed. He had too much speed, and hitting me had thrown his balance off. I watched as he tried to maneuver himself into a power-slide, but he couldn't get control. One of his front wheels hit a stone. He shot toward the edge of the road, onto the gravel, and was launched off his board.

He shot right over the side of the cliff.

chapter thirteen

"Goat!" I yelled. My clothes were torn, and there were cuts and scrapes all over my arms and legs. I got up and fell back down as my right knee gave out. I couldn't tell if my knee was broken, strained or what. But it hurt, and my leg couldn't hold any of my weight. I stumbled over to the edge of the road where Goat had gone off. It was a straight drop into thick forest. I yelled down into the darkness.

"Goat! Are you all right?" There was no response. I looked around, trying to figure out what to do. "Goat!" I yelled again. I couldn't see anything but trees. How could he not be dead? I couldn't even tell how far down the cliff dropped. I heard the screech of rusty brakes, and Jack came sliding to a stop beside me.

"Wow, this is a crazy ride," he said, smiling. His hair had blown across his forehead and was damp from the rain. He looked down at Goat's long board. "Hey, where's Goat?"

"He went over the cliff," I said. I felt as if I was going to be sick. "He flew right off. His board caught on the gravel, and he just..."

"Crap!" Jack said, dropping his bike. "Goat!" No response. He yelled again. "What are we supposed to do?"

"Call someone," I said.

"I left my phone in my car," Jack said. "Where's yours?"

I pulled my phone out of my pocket. The phone flashed on and off again.

I remembered flopping onto my bed the night before and forgetting to charge it. "Dead."

"What are we supposed to do?" Jack said again.

"We have to go down there. He could be hurt. Or dead."

"No," Jack said. "We have to get to the bottom and get help!"

"If he's hurt, we have to help him now. He could be bleeding down there."

Jack was motionless. I guess he had never been in a situation like this, one that was real. One where he actually had to *do* something, not call someone else to do it for him. He looked over the edge of the cliff and yelled again.

No answer.

"How are we even going to get down there?" he asked.

I looked over the edge of the cliff. The rock face was smooth, slick, and plunged straight down. "I don't know."

There didn't seem to be any way to climb down. We walked along the edge of the road, calling Goat's name over and over. No response.

A gust of wind blew rain across our faces, and the trees swayed.

"Anything?" Jack called from farther down the road.

"No. It's sheer rock everywhere."

"Nothing here either," he called back. "Goat!" he yelled into the forest below. He joined me at the spot where Goat had gone over. He looked pale. "What are we going to do?"

I didn't know. All I knew was we had to get to Goat as soon as possible. I looked over the edge again. "Maybe we can climb down one of these trees," I said. I reached out and touched the end of a long branch. There had to be a ledge or a landing of some kind below. Either that or the trees were hundreds of feet high. "We just have to swing across on one of these branches, grab hold of the trunk and climb down."

"No way, man," Jack said. "What if I fall?"

"Listen, Jack, none of us would be out here right now if it wasn't for you."

"Don't hang this on me, man. I never forced anyone into doing anything. Goat came to me with the idea–"

"And you could have said no, but you didn't. So I had to do these stupid competitions with Goat. Don't you see that? I didn't have a choice, Jack. Not all of us are big movie stars who don't have to worry about anything. But you wouldn't understand, would you? Everything is a game to you," I said.

"That's not true. I wanted the best trainer and stunt double, that's all."

"You already had him," I said. "None of this had to happen. Goat's five inches taller than you. Is it even possible for him to be your stunt double?"

"Sure, well, maybe."

I was tired of Jack Coagen. He was never going to understand what I was talking about. The guy shot his first film when he was four. What did he know about trying to make a life for himself? Everything had always been handed to him.

"I don't get you," I said. It was getting darker by the minute. Soon we would need flashlights to find Goat. "Listen, you can stay here if you want. I'm going to climb down and try to help Goat." I fixed my eyes on the nearest tree. The branches were thin but long, and the trunk wasn't more than five feet away. If I jumped, I could grab one of the branches and swing to the trunk. I stepped back and bumped into Jack. "Move. I have to get a run at this," I said.

Jack looked at me and then looked at the tree. "You think you can make that jump?"

I clapped my hands together. They still burned from my wipeout. My knee hurt, too, although it wasn't broken, probably only bruised. I was still hobbling, but I could run and jump across to the tree. I hoped.

"I have to try," I said. I was about to start running when Jack put his arm out in front of me.

"Wait," he said.

"What?"

He pointed to a different tree. "That one is closer. And there aren't as many branches."

I looked where he was pointing. He was right. The other tree was a better option. Plus the trunk looked thicker. I walked toward the edge.

"Let me go first," Jack said.

"What?"

"You're right. I got you into this. Both of you." He brushed past me and lined himself up with the tree. "Plus, you're hurt."

Before I could say anything, he leaned forward and, in one swift motion, ran to the edge of the road and jumped. He flew through the air, his arms outstretched before him, and disappeared into the branches of the tree.

chapter fourteen

"You all right?" I yelled. He didn't say anything. "Jack!"

"Yeah, yeah, I'm all right. Just got the wind knocked out of me."

I squinted into the darkness. I could just barely make out his form clinging to the trunk of the tree.

"It's not that bad," Jack said. "But you have to be ready for it. I'll yell when I get to the bottom."

"All right." Branches snapped as Jack climbed down the tree. I felt as if I was standing alone at the edge of the world. "You down yet, Jack?" I yelled. There was no response and my heart started to beat faster. "Jack!"

"Yeah, yeah," he said. "The branches at the bottom of this tree are thick. Come down slowly. The jump isn't that far. You'll be able to make it."

"Okay," I said. "Look out. I'm going to throw my board down." I heaved the board over and listened to it breaking branches the whole way down. I hoped it wouldn't land on Goat. I leaned forward and ran, jumping at the last possible moment.

It was exhilarating, leaping through the air, but painful when I hit the tree. I wrapped my arms around the trunk and tried to catch my breath.

"You okay?" Jack yelled.

"Yeah," I said. I placed my foot on the first branch I could reach. I shifted over, put my other foot on a branch. The branch creaked and groaned, but it held. I looked down and all I could see was darkness.

"You see Goat anywhere?" I said.

"I'm waiting for you," Jack said. "It's really dark down here."

I shifted down another couple of branches and felt as if I was entering another world. "You see my board?" I asked, wanting to hear Jack's voice again.

"Yeah. Yeah, I got it right here."

I slid down a few more branches. One smacked against my face, and I checked to see if I had been cut. I felt the gash on my forehead and pulled my hand back to find blood on my fingers. "Crap," I said.

"What?" Jack's voice sounded closer, but I still couldn't tell how far away the ground was.

I slid down another couple of branches. "Nothing. I just cut myself." I put my foot on the next branch and heard a snap. A moment later I was free-falling. I landed on the ground, a tangle of arms and legs.

"Casey, are you okay?" Jack asked.

I nodded and tried to roll over. I had only fallen a couple of feet, but I had landed weirdly. I gasped for air, coughed a few times and inhaled. "Yeah," I said. I got up on one knee. It *was* really dark down here. There were funnels of light from above where the trees thinned. It was quiet too. Very quiet.

"Which way should we go?" Jack asked.

"Just a second," I said. I worked at breathing properly again. Then I waited until my eyes adjusted to the darkness. Jack stood in front of me and ran his hand through his hair.

"Man, he could be anywhere down here," said Jack. "He could be dead."

I slowly stood up but had to stay crouched over. My whole body felt bruised. "We need to search along the side of the cliff. He has to be near the edge somewhere." We were standing on more than just a ledge. It looked as if we were actually at the top of a long, steep hill.

"All right, let's see if we can find him," Jack said.

Neither of us moved. There was a chance Goat was dead. It was a long fall, and he'd shot straight down. "Yeah," I said. "Yeah, let's get started." I tucked my long board under my arm.

"Oh, man," Jack said. "I hope he's alive."

"Same here." We hadn't walked more than ten feet when I spotted something on the ground.

A foot.

It was bare, and its whiteness cut through the dark foliage.

"Crap," I said, coming to a stop.

Jack bumped into me. "What?"

"There he is." We stared down at Goat. His right leg was bent under him. The left one stuck out in front of his body, and his shoe was missing. His head tilted awkwardly to one side, and his eyes were closed.

He looked dead.

Really dead.

"Is he alive?" Jack asked.

"I don't know."

"Well, check."

I took a deep breath and knelt beside Goat. Blood was seeping out of his pant leg, and his right wrist was bent back at a strange angle. It looked as if he had crashed through the branches right to the ground. There was a skid mark in the leaves behind him.

"Is he alive?" Jack said again.

I didn't reply. What if he was dead? What if this stupid competition had killed him?

"Casey," Jack said. "Is he alive?"

I finally put two fingers on Goat's neck, which was exactly when he sat up and sucked in a giant gulp of air.

chapter fifteen

"Goat!" I yelled.

He stared at me as if he had no idea who I was. Then he reached for his right leg and fell back, screaming. "What the hell!" he yelled and closed his eyes.

"It's all right, Goat. You're all right," I said.

His hands came away from his leg with blood on them, and he screamed again. "What the hell happened!"

Jack knelt on the other side of him. "It's all right. We're here," Jack said in a strange, almost motherly voice. "You took a fall."

Goat stared at him, blank-faced. "Oh, man, I went right off that cliff."

"You did," I said.

He closed his eyes. "I must have hit a dozen branches on the way down." He looked up at me. "How am I still alive?"

"I don't know," I said. "You think you can stand?" He didn't move. I wasn't sure if he hadn't heard me, or if he was too freaked-out to answer. "Goat, do you think you can stand?"

"I don't know. It feels like there's something wrong with my ankle."

"Try moving," Jack said.

Goat gently pulled his right leg out from under himself. He winced. "That really...arggg...hurts. My wrist as well. I can't feel my fingers. And it's hard to breathe." His face was completely white. He shook his head and said, "Stupid, stupid, stupid."

"Do you have your phone?" I asked.

"Where's yours?" he said.

"The battery's dead. And Jack left his in his car. Man, where's that paparazzi guy when you need him?"

Goat looked at Jack. "Where's your skateboard?"

"In my car, why?" Jack said.

Goat sighed. "Because that's how the paparazzi guy was finding you."

"What?" Jack said.

"My phone's in my pocket," Goat said to me. "Front one. You'll have to get it. I can't move my hand."

I reached into his pocket and felt the broken bits of what had previously been Goat's phone. I pulled it out in case the battery happened to be the same as mine. It wasn't.

"The skateboard I gave you had a GPS tracker on it," Goat said. "That's how the photographer was able to locate you."

"What the hell?" Jack said. "You put a GPS tracker on my skateboard?"

"Your agent told me to. He was the one who set all of this up."

"Why?" Jack said. He was still kneeling beside Goat.

Goat closed his eyes. "He said some of the producers were thinking of pulling out of the film and taking their money with them. They don't think you're going to make it as a non-kid actor."

"So what does that have to do with the photographer?" I said.

"Jack's agent asked me to get his face in the tabloids. He wanted dirty shots. Like the one of Jack in a fight at the party. And that one of the cop holding on to him at the park the other day."

"So that was all a setup? That girl claiming I had assaulted her?" Jack said.

"Yeah. She's a friend of mine. She told the cops someone had knocked her over and grabbed her arm and stuff. She said she thought it was you, but that she wasn't certain. So the cops brought her to the park to ID you. Once the photographer had taken the pictures he needed, she told the cops it wasn't you. But by then, the story was out about you being questioned on an assault case."

"Man, that is low," Jack said. He stood up and took a couple of steps back. "Why would my agent do that?"

"I paid McNaughton to harass you too," Goat said. "To try and get you in a fight or something. Anything for a good photo opportunity."

"Goat," I said. "Can you stand? We have to get out of here."

Goat sat up. He touched his right leg and cringed. "I think it's broken. I can't move anything from my knee down. It hurts too much." He put his left hand on the ground behind him and fell back. "And my wrist too. Man, I think it's broken as well." There was no easy way to get back to the road. There was only one way for us to get out of here, and that was down the hill.

I put my long board on the ground. "Do you think you can sit on our hands if we cross them into a chairlift?" I said.

Goat raised his head, and we helped him sit up. He leaned against Jack. We slid our hands underneath his butt and tried to lift him.

We could only raise him a foot off the ground. Goat was breathing strangely. Kind of gasping and then exhaling slowly. "This is not going to work," Jack said.

We put Goat back down. "Are you all right, Goat?" I said.

He shook his head. "I told you, I can't breathe right. It hurts every time I inhale."

"That's not good," Jack said.

"No," I said. "Goat. We're going to have to get you down the hill."

"But I can't walk," he said. His voice was quivering. He sounded terrified, like a little kid who's lost in a mall and can't find his mom.

"Goat, no one is going to come and get us. The only person who even knows we're up here is Sara, and she went to her grandparents. Unless you told someone?" I said.

"No," Goat said.

"No one at all?" I asked.

"No, man. I didn't think it was something we should advertise."

I looked down the slope into the darkness. Night had settled around us, and with the thick storm clouds and rain, no moonlight reached us.

I knelt down beside him. "We'll have to carry you. It's our only choice, Goat. It's going to get colder soon. We don't have a phone, and no one uses that road at this time of year." He looked at me, and I could tell he was on the verge of crying. "We're not going to leave you here." His lips were quivering, and his eyes were glassy. I grabbed his arm and threw it over my shoulder.

"Jack," I said. "Get the other side." Jack got under Goat's other arm and we slowly raised Goat up again. He immediately sagged forward, causing us to stumble a couple of steps and fall. Goat screamed as his injured wrist and leg hit the ground.

"It's not going to work, Casey," Jack said. "He's too tall, and he can't hold himself up." I looked around for something to help us and grabbed my long board.

"Here," I said, crouching down beside Jack. "Hold the other end of this. Goat can sit on it."

Jack grabbed the board, and we helped Goat slide onto it.

"Put your arms around our necks, Goat. All right. Now, Jack, get up slowly," I said once Goat was settled in the middle of the deck. Goat was heavy, and holding the board was awkward. "Good," I said. "All right. One step at a time."

It was going to be a very, very long walk.

chapter sixteen

We had no idea how long a walk it was to the base of the mountain. It felt as though we were walking endlessly over the same ground. Luckily we had the slope of the hill to guide us. Otherwise we would have ended up walking in circles.

Goat groaned occasionally but was mostly silent. His weight became more and more difficult to manage. Every ten minutes we had to set the board on the ground and rest. I rubbed my knee, which was feeling worse from bearing Goat's weight.

"This is going to take forever," Jack said. "Maybe one of us should go get help and come back."

"How would we do that, Jack? Leave a trail of bread crumbs? It's dark, and there's no way to know where we are."

"I don't know. It's not like I've ever been in a situation like this before." Goat was laid out on the ground between us, breathing in quick bursts.

"Why would your agent do all this?" I asked.

"What? The paparazzi stuff?"

"Sure. And getting someone to make it look like you're in trouble with the police." Jack wrapped his arms around himself and stared at the ground. We were both shivering from the cold.

"He's my new agent," Jack said. "My parents thought I needed someone fresh to help break into the regular film market. He's one of the best."

"He sounds like an ass."

"It's just the way he does business. The press, actors, directors–everyone knows this is how some agents work."

I rubbed my knee, which felt as though it was seizing up. I wanted to lie down, but I knew I wouldn't be able to get back up again if I did. "It all seems so fake," I said.

"Sure it does," Jack said.

"So it doesn't bother you?" I asked.

"What, getting all that publicity? You know what they say, 'no publicity is bad publicity.'"

"But it's not just publicity, right? I mean, you get accused of assaulting a girl, and people are going to think you would actually do something like that."

"No, they won't. They might think that for a few days, until the real story comes out. And if people still thought I had done it, I would go on a talk show and say how disappointed I am about the situation and I had nothing to do with it. Then everyone sees I'm really a nice guy that got shafted, which makes me look even better."

I couldn't understand any of it. And I wasn't certain I even wanted to be a part of this make-believe world. "We have to keep going," I said, standing and stretching my leg out. I felt unbelievably tired, as though I could sleep for days.

"Okay," Jack said, nodding his head. "All right. Let's keep going."

We hoisted Goat up again and started moving. All three of us were shivering. The light rain had soaked our clothes through. We walked for about two minutes before a thick band of trees stopped us.

"Which way?" Jack said.

"Let's go this way," I said, nodding to the left. As we turned, Jack caught his foot on a root and slipped. The board came out of my hands and Goat fell hard to the ground. Other than the thud of his body hitting the earth, he barely made a sound.

"Goat," I said, shaking him. "Goat." There was no response. He'd fallen forward and was lying with his face in the mud. "Help me roll him over," I said to Jack. I grabbed Goat's shoulders, and Jack grabbed his legs. We gently rolled him onto his back. His eyes were still closed. I rubbed the mud off his face and put my ear to his mouth. He was breathing, but it sounded thin and weak. "He doesn't look good," I said.

"There's a lot of blood down here," Jack said.

I looked at Goat's leg. His pant leg was soaked with blood, and more was seeping onto the ground.

"What are we going to do?" Jack asked. "He's going to die out here. This isn't working. I can't carry him anymore."

"What other choice do we have?" I said.

"I don't know!"

I wanted to start screaming "Help! Help!" over and over again. But who would hear us? I took a deep breath. "We have to keep going. At least until we can find some kind of marker."

"What do you mean?"

"Like a really big tree or a path or *something*. Then one of us can run and get help."

"He's completely out, Casey. It's like dragging dead weight."

"Come on, help me get him up." We sat there for a moment, holding Goat. I heard scurrying in the woods and remembered this was prime coyote territory. Jack got in behind Goat and held him forward. I flung one of his arms over my shoulders and sat him back on the board. "All right, get on the other side and lift him."

Jack reached for Goat's other arm, and together we lifted him off the ground and back onto the long board.

"He's too heavy," Jack said.

"No, he's not. Come on, we can do this." There was more wrong with Goat than a broken ankle or wrist. His breathing was irregular, and blood dripped off his pant leg. If we didn't get him down the mountain soon, there was a good chance he wouldn't survive. "One step at a time, Jack. That's all we have to do."

We stumbled forward. The forest thickened, making it difficult to keep the long board level. We didn't talk much except to give each other directions on how to navigate around a tree or to watch out for a thick root. The incline was leveling out, which probably meant we were nearing the bottom. But there was no way to know for sure.

"Let's put him down again," Jack said.

"In a minute," I said. I was afraid if I stopped, I wouldn't be able to stand up again, but I didn't want Jack to know. He was freaked-out enough already.

"I can't hold him," Jack said. "I'm going to drop him."

I kept walking. "No, you're not. You're going to keep carrying him."

Jack closed his eyes and clenched his jaw.

"You can do this, Jack." We climbed over a series of large rocks and found a trail of sorts. "Wait a second," I said.

Jack stopped. He looked down. "Is this a trail?"

"Yeah," I said. "I think I see something up ahead."

"What? Where?"

"A field," I said. "Over there. Come on, you can make it that far."

"I can't, Casey. He's too heavy."

"We don't have a choice, Jack. We have to get Goat out of here. If we stop, Goat dies." Even before the words were out of my mouth, I knew they were true.

chapter seventeen

We shuffled down the trail. My arms were killing me. The rain had subsided, and a break in the clouds let enough moonlight through to wash the field in a hazy, silver glow. There was a fence around the field and a long cement water trough off to one side. "Let's get him over there," I said, nodding toward the fence. We carried Goat a few more feet and then set him down with his back against the fence.

He still hadn't opened his eyes, and his skin was pale gray. I looked across the field for a farmhouse or some other structure.

Jack flopped down beside Goat. "Now what?" he said.

I didn't know where we were or which direction would take me to a road. The clearing was surrounded by forest. Why was there a field here? I slid the long board out from under Goat. "I'll go get help," I said.

"And leave us here?" Jack said. He looked at Goat. "What if he dies?"

"He's not going to die," I said, bending down close to Jack. "Because we're going to save him." Jack stared at me. "You have to wait here, Jack. We can't leave him alone. I'll be back as soon as I can with help." I stood up and scanned the edges of the field. There had to be a path leading to it.

"Hurry up, all right?" said Jack.

"I will. I promise." I climbed over the fence and kept moving so my knee wouldn't seize. It ached, and a hot pain shot through it with every step.

I circled the perimeter of the fence looking for a gate. Three-quarters of the way around, I spotted a gap in the tree line and what looked like another path. Farther along, I found a break in the fence. I stepped through it and started to run as fast as my knee would allow.

The path was wide and snaked all over. Almost immediately, it cut back up the hill. I didn't want to be climbing. My knee didn't want me to be climbing. It felt as if I might be backtracking. But there was no other way to go, and I wasn't about to turn around. The trail had to lead somewhere. All I could do was follow it.

I had no idea what time it was or how long we'd been out in the forest, and I was exhausted. I needed to find help. I kept moving as best I could, dodging roots and rocks. The long board became heavier with every step. I was tempted to leave it on the side of the path. But what if I found a road ahead? It would be easier to skate than walk.

I slowed down to catch my breath. Being alone was scary. I could hear animals moving in the darkness. The trail was extremely narrow in some places, and I veered into the forest several times and had to find my way back out again.

A ridge jutted to the right. I stumbled over the top, tripped on something, and the next thing I knew, I was rolling down a mud-slick hill. I let go of the board, jammed my feet into the ground and came to a stop.

"Crap!" I yelled. My pant leg was torn, and my sore knee was bleeding. It was only a scrape, but it hurt even more than before. I sat down, stared at the blood oozing from my knee and felt like crying. What was I doing out here? Would I ever be a stunt double? What did Jack's agent's word mean when he obviously lacked any morals? Sara had been right. This whole thing was stupid and dangerous.

The trail looked as if it would keep going and going. I could be miles from a road. Maybe the trail didn't even meet up with a road. Maybe it was part of a giant web of trails through the woods. It was impossible to know. I tried to stand, and my knee gave out, dumping me back on the ground. I lay there with the back of my head in the mud and the rain pricking my face. I was in pain, but it didn't feel like I had any cracked bones. I heard a rustling in the woods behind me and used the long board as a makeshift crutch to stand. I grabbed a long stick with my other hand to use as a weapon in case an animal came out of the woods.

Then I took a step.

And another.

And another.

"This is all you have to do, Casey," I said to myself. "You have to keep going." The ground was muddy, and my foot slipped with each step.

I managed to cover ten feet before I stopped, dropped the stick and leaned against a tree to catch my breath. I was staring at the ground when I heard something. Not an animal in the woods, but something else. I listened carefully. It sounded like a stream, like water moving over rocks. But then it stopped. Streams don't stop. I listened harder, but there was nothing. I pushed off the tree, took a few steps, and then there it was again–the whooshing sound of water flowing over earth or–tires on wet pavement!

chapter eighteen

I squinted into the darkness. It had to be a road. And it couldn't be far. Maybe it was a hundred feet away? Start walking and count your steps, I told myself.

One.

Two.

"Help!" I yelled.

Three.

Four.

"I need help!" I leaned into the trail, jammed the long board into the ground in front of me and took another step. I saw the flash of headlights on trees.

"Keep going," I said. "Just. Keep. Going." I put my head down, determined not to look up until I reached the road. The incline wasn't very steep, but every step was a battle. The mud either sucked at my shoes or sent me sliding back down. I jammed the long board into the ground and used it like a claw to pull myself up the hill. My knee burned with white-hot pain. I gritted my teeth and heaved myself forward, trying not to think about the possibility that a nearby road was an illusion.

And then I looked up to find I was standing on the edge of a road that cut through the forest and curved downhill. Lights glowed at the bottom, a faint smudge of civilization in the distance.

I had no idea where I was. But it didn't matter. I looked back at the trail and tried to find a marker of some kind. A guardrail ended fifteen feet farther up the road. It wasn't distinct in any way, but I thought

I could remember what it looked like when I came back with help.

I waited a couple of minutes for another car to pass. Nothing. It was the middle of the night, and this wasn't downtown LA. It could be hours before another car passed.

I checked where the trail was again, dropped my long board and put my foot on it. It felt as if someone had stabbed me in the knee. I bent over to squeeze and massage it. Then I tried again. I pushed once and quickly placed my back foot on the board. Then I knelt as close to the board as possible and let gravity do the rest.

The hill wasn't very steep, so I didn't pick up an unreasonable amount of speed. But soon enough I was cruising along faster than I wished. It was hard to steer. I considered sitting on the board, but sitting down would require stopping first. With my leg as it was, the only way for me to stop would be to bail, which would seriously hurt. So I kept going.

I rounded three corners, the wheels whipping along on the slick pavement.

And then the road went straight down, and the glow I'd seen in the distance materialized into a line of streetlights and a flashing yellow traffic light.

I rolled to a stop beneath the blinking yellow light. I looked up and down the road and couldn't see any cars or houses. The wind whistled through the trees, and rain from the leaves splattered across the ground. I looked to the left and didn't recognize anything. But something about the opposite direction seemed familiar, and there were more streetlights that way.

I dropped my board and pushed. Everything in my body protested as I pushed again and again until the board glided into the next intersection. There was a pizza place, a dry cleaner and a convenience store, but they were all closed. Still no houses anywhere. And not a pay phone in sight.

"Help!" I yelled, my voice echoing off the buildings. I rolled through the intersection. Then I looked back at the mountain and noticed a sign on the side of the road.

Beacon Hill Road, Authorized Personnel Only. I turned around and skated with a new burst of energy along the quiet, empty street. I knew exactly where I was. I turned a corner and there it was, right where we'd left it: Jack's Lexus.

And beside it, the photographer's gray Toyota.

I rolled over to the Toyota and banged on the window. The photographer jumped and hit the wheel. The horn blared. "What the hell?" he said. He opened the door and got out, rubbing his eyes. "Where did you come from?"

"The woods." I pointed up the road. "Goat's hurt. Jack's with him."

"What? Who?"

"Goat. Fraser Gauthier." It seemed strange to use Goat's real name. I couldn't remember the last time I'd called him Fraser.

"Where?"

"Back up the road. Call the police or an ambulance or something." The photographer looked confused, but he pulled out his cell phone and dialed 9-1-1. He spoke to someone and then stayed on the line. "Get in," he said, pointing to the passenger door.

I hopped over on one foot, opened the back door and slid my long board in along the floor. I got in the passenger's side and leaned back heavily in the seat.

The photographer jumped in and started the car. "You don't look so good," he said.

"I don't feel so good."

"What happened?"

I didn't feel like telling him everything. I didn't feel like talking at all. I couldn't remember ever being so tired. "We were racing down Beacon Hill, and Goat went off a cliff."

"Is he all right?"

I looked over at the guy. "No." I sucked back some tears and felt a hot burn at the back of my throat. "We have to hurry, please. The two of them are stuck in the bush. I think there's something really wrong with Goat. I mean, Fraser."

"Which way?" he said.

I pointed back the way I had come. He put in his Bluetooth and took off. I stared at the road, hoping I would recognize where I had come out of the forest and onto the road.

chapter nineteen

"Were you here waiting for Jack?" I asked the photographer. It was dark inside his car. In any other situation, I would have been freaked-out about being in a car with some guy I didn't know. But at the moment it didn't matter. To be able to sit was enough. Hot air poured from the vents. I held my hands up to them. It felt as if I would never be warm again.

"Yeah, I thought it was strange that his car was parked there," the photographer said.

"You were waiting for Jack to come back, so you could get some photos?" I asked.

"Exactly," he replied. Jack was nothing to him. A job.

"Where are they?" he asked.

"In a field in the middle of the woods."

"How are we going to find them?"

"There's a trail," I said.

"One of them is Jack Coagen," the photographer said to the 9-1-1 operator. "Yeah, the kid actor."

The Toyota's headlights illuminated the guardrail, and I spotted a cut in the tree line. "Right there," I said, pointing toward the path into the trees. The photographer pulled the car over.

"We're there now. Can you trace my phone?" The photographer listened for a moment and then said, "Okay, sure, I'll stay on the line." He looked over at me.

"You'll likely get some shots of him tonight," I said.

"Really?" he said.

I nodded, closed my eyes and tried to stretch out.

"The kid says they're back in the bush somewhere," the photographer said to the 9-1-1 operator. "So, I guess, bring whatever you need to get people out of the bush." He looked over at me. "How far in are they?"

"I don't know," I said. It felt as if it had taken months to get out of the forest. "A long way."

The photographer relayed this information as the flashing lights of a cruiser approached and lit up the interior of the car. When the cruiser stopped behind us, the photographer opened his door. "I'll be right back, kid. You wait here."

I heard his feet on the gravel and doors slamming. And then I went somewhere else. I stared at the road and thought about everything that had happened. It seemed enough to fill a month of my life, but it had only been one night.

The door opened, and an officer stuck his head inside. "Where are they?" he asked. He had a two-way radio in his hand. The voices coming from it sounded like a whole army unit was involved.

"Straight along that trail," I said. "Eventually you come to a fenced-in field, if that makes sense."

"That's McConnell's field." He yelled some instructions to the other officer and then brought the two-way radio to his face. "Send a chopper in. They're in McConnell's field. That'll be the only way to get them out." He stuck his head back in the car. "That field is a stop point for horseback riders. That's a long way in, kid. You sure you're all right?"

"I'm getting there," I said.

"What were you kids doing up there anyway?" he asked.

I didn't know what to say. I shrugged, knowing the truth of what we had been doing would all come out eventually.

"Skating Beacon Hill Road," I said.

The officer looked at me sternly. "You know that road is closed to any traffic." I nodded. "And you know a kid died skateboarding down there not long ago." I nodded again. "So why would you do it?"

I looked at the ground. "I guess I didn't think I had a choice."

"Of course you had a choice," the officer said. "Did someone hold a gun to your head and say, 'Throw yourself down this hill'?"

"No."

The officer banged the roof of the car with his palm. "Someday you'll learn you always have a choice, kid. It's part of being an adult to make the right one."

I nodded. It was likely true. The problem was, I didn't always feel like I had a choice.

"An ambulance is on the way. Someone will check you out. I'll be back to talk to you after that." He shut the door, and I closed my eyes.

There was a lot of commotion. I listened to it like I listen to the television when I'm half-asleep. The voices were distant, then close up. I closed my eyes and let everything wash over me. People were taking care of things now. People who knew what to do. People who didn't get into stupid situations and not know how to get out of them.

When the door finally opened again, I almost fell out of the car.

"Whoa there," someone said. I felt hands on my arm. "You okay? Can you speak to me?" I opened my eyes. The guy holding me up had tightly clipped blond hair and glasses. He smiled and tilted his head. "Anyone home?"

"Sure," I said.

"What hurts?"

"Everything," I said. He pulled my pant leg apart and looked at the cut on my knee.

"This is really swollen," he said. He reached behind him and grabbed an ice pack. "Here, hold this there. Do you think you can walk to the ambulance?"

I looked over at the ambulance. It seemed very far away. I've already come this far, I thought. "Sure," I said. "Why not." I shifted in my seat, placed my feet on the ground and stood.

chapter twenty

Jack, Goat and I had been in the forest together for almost six hours. It was close to two in the morning when I found the road, and nearly four by the time they managed to get Goat and Jack out. The photographer had hiked in to meet the helicopter crew and took dozens of photos. Photos of Jack holding Goat up. Jack waving from the ground, his arms a giant Y. Jack with Goat's arm over his shoulder. Jack being tended to by a paramedic. Within days, they were splashed across the Internet and on the covers of the kinds of magazines found in grocery-store checkouts. Jack Coagen was a hero. Or so it would seem in the papers anyway.

The photographer took a few shots of me that night, too, but I asked him not to print them. I knew what had happened out there. I knew what we had been through. I didn't need the world to congratulate me. And I didn't need the publicity.

Three days after the rescue, I went to visit Goat in the hospital. I didn't ask about his injuries. He looked as if he was in pain from one end of his body to the other. He was sitting up, watching a movie on a little television when I came in his room.

"Head Case."

"Goat," I said. I wasn't sure where to sit. There was a chair beside Goat's bed, but it seemed too close to him, and there was junk piled on it.

"What are you doing here?" he said.

I decided to move the junk and sat down. "Just wanted to make sure you were still breathing."

"I am."

"Cool," I said. "All right, I guess I'll be going then." I stood and started toward the door.

"Sit down, Casey," Goat said. He coughed, grabbed at his side and lay his head on the pillow with a sigh.

"Okay," I said, returning to the chair.

"I'm going to be in here a while, apparently."

"Yeah?"

"Yeah. I need a couple of surgeries." I didn't know what to say. "Nothing really serious, but I guess my insides got kind of messed up," he added.

"Well, flying off a twenty-foot drop tends to do that," I said.

Goat smiled. "Listen." He looked back at the television. "Listen, I'm sorry about all this."

I glanced out the window. "Are you?"

"It was stupid. But, man, you've got everything. And it just seemed like you were getting one more thing, and, I don't know...What do I have?"

I had no idea what he was talking about. "What are you saying, Goat?"

"You're smart, you're likely going to college. And you're a better skater than I am. There, I said it. It's true. It's just comes naturally for you. I have to work at it all the time. And even though she bugs me, you've got a cool girlfriend."

"Sara? She's not my girlfriend."

Goat looked at me and smirked. "She's not?"

"No."

"Can I have her phone number then?"

Something inside me riled up at the thought of Goat and Sara together. "No," I said.

He smiled. "Maybe you should do something about that, man. Anyway, I said it. I'm sorry. It was stupid."

"It was, and, in the end, you're the one that got hurt."

"Go figure," he said.

A nurse came into the room with a tray. At first I thought she was bringing food, but when she set the tray on the bedside table, I saw the needles and pills.

"And that's my cue to get out of here," I said. I extended my hand toward him. "I would say no hard feelings, but we almost killed one another out there."

Goat took my hand and shook it. "Good luck with the movie," he said.

The nurse flicked her finger against the needle. I shivered and walked out of the room before she lifted Goat's sleeve up.

When I got home, there were two messages on my answering machine. One was from Jack, the other one was from Sara. I called Jack back.

"Casey," he said. "I tried your cell, but it said it was no longer in service."

"Yeah, I haven't paid my bill."

"Oh." There was a long pause in which I could hear a lot of people talking in the background and then an announcement over a loudspeaker.

"Where are you?"

"Oh, I'm on set. Actually, it's the preliminary shots for the skate movie." There was another long pause. "So, are you still interested in helping me?"

I thought about it. After everything I had been through, was I still interested in being a stunt double?

"When do you start shooting?" I asked.

"It looks like next week. The director has another guy in mind for the stunt stuff, but I'll push him if you still want the job." There was another pause. Then Jack said, "I would understand if you don't want anything to do with it."

"When do I have to let you know?" I asked.

"Sometime this week. Take your time."

"All right. I'll call you soon."

"And, Casey?"

"Yeah?"

"I'm sorry about...Well, you know, about everything."

"That's all right, Jack."

"Cool. We'll be talking," he said and hung up.

I stared out my kitchen window and hit *Play* on the answering machine again. I listened to Sara's message and decided not to call her back. I knew where she would be anyway.

It was a warm September afternoon. The sun shone high and bright above the half-pipe.

I climbed the ramp and sat with my back to the railing. Three guys I knew were there. We talked for a few minutes, and then I started to worry Sara wouldn't show. I was about to ask one of the guys if I could borrow his cell phone when Sara walked out of the break in the trees and started across the parking lot. She tucked her board under her arm, stopped at the bottom of the ramp and looked up at me.

"You didn't call me back," she said.

"I decided to just come here."

"I was sitting by my phone, sinking deeply into depression."

"I imagine you were."

"You could go back and forth in here forever if you wanted to," she said.

"You could." My knee was feeling better, but not good enough to ride a ramp.

"And that should be enough, right?" she said.

"Right," I said.

"Wrong," she said, with a smile. "But it would be something." Then she dropped in.

I thought about how she was moving away to go to college in the next few days. These endless days of skating and hanging out would soon end. It made me anxious. I hadn't applied to any colleges yet, so I had decided to take Jack up on his offer and do the stunt-double gig. But I would do it my way this time. I never wanted to feel at the mercy of someone else again. I would do what I loved, and I would do it on my terms.

I watched her ride the half-pipe with a big smile on her face. I listened to her wheels rolling, the tap of her board as it struck the coping, and then I closed my eyes. The ocean breeze brushed over me, and I thought, Yeah, it was something.

Acknowledgments

Special thanks to Megan Ross, my first reader and muse; Sara Finlay and Danny McNaughton for donating their awesome names; my kids for hanging out with me while I skateboard so I don't look as ridiculous; Christi Howes for sprucing this mess up, and Sarah Harvey for steering it in the right direction in the first place; OnDeck Skateboard Shop in Ottawa and Broken Skateboards; and finally, for all the thirty- and forty-somethings who refuse to grow up and who help keep sports like skateboarding and snowboarding alive and vibrant.

Jeff Ross grew up near Collingwood, Ontario, where he learned to snowboard, skateboard and injure himself in fantastic and unique ways. Jeff lives in Ottawa, Ontario, where he teaches English and Scriptwriting at Algonquin College. *Powerslide* is his second novel for the Orca Sports series. More information is available at www.jeffrossbooks.com.

Titles in the Series

orca sports

Absolute Pressure
Sigmund Brouwer

All-Star Pride
Sigmund Brouwer

Blazer Drive
Sigmund Brouwer

Boarder Patrol
Erin Thomas

Chief Honor
Sigmund Brouwer

Cobra Strike
Sigmund Brouwer

Crossover
Jeff Rud

Dead in the Water
Robin Stevenson

The Drop
Jeff Ross

Fly Away
Nora Rock

Flying Feet
James McCann

Gravity Check
Alex Van Tol

Hitmen Triumph
Sigmund Brouwer

Hurricane Power
Sigmund Brouwer

Jumper
Michele Martin Bossley

Kicker
Michele Martin Bossley

Maverick Mania
Sigmund Brouwer

Oil King Courage
Sigmund Brouwer

Paralyzed
Jeff Rud

Powerslide
Jeff Ross

Razor's Edge
Nikki Tate

Rebel Glory
Sigmund Brouwer